Blueberries and Other Stories

Femdom Mind Control

Flash Fiction – Vol. 29

S.B.

Table of Contents

Have a bite of mindless pleasure.

My sincerest thanks to all patrons of Spell... B-O-U-N-D.

A Distraction

Mildred almost spat her drink when she saw her father hump the kitchen chair like a dog in heat. The retired gym teacher had always been a rational soul averse to any kind of fun outside the book, yet hypnosis awakened a side of him no one knew he had.

"Isn't it funny?" Her younger sister, Jane, asked. The freckled redhead that loved everything related with altered states of mind had recently returned from a long trek across Europe with a few new tricks up her sleeve, and she couldn't waste a good opportunity to show them off.

"It's something, that's for sure. You've got really good at this."

Both women sat together at their father's house, drinking ginger tea. It was the day of his sixty-sixth birthday and things had escalated quickly from a simple cake and candles. If their mother were still alive, she would have approved the turn of events, but some things aren't meant to be.

"Thank you, sis. It wouldn't have worked if he wasn't such a good subject, though. When is your turn?"

"Never. I don't want you poking around here, sorry."

"Why not?"

"Who knows what sort of inappropriate things you would have me do while I was under? I'm not taking that chance."

"That's not how this works. I can't make you do anything you don't want to do"

"So, do you seriously expect me to believe that dad secretly wanted to fuck a chair like there's no tomorrow? Not buying that. There's more to this story you're not telling me."

"Okay, I suppose it's possible to slowly change one's desires through repeated conditioning, but it takes a lot of time to get there. Here's a secret: this wasn't the first time I entranced Dad."

"What? How many times then?"

"I'm not sure, but we started a few months ago. He was going through another slump following mom's death, so I gave his mind something else to be distracted with."

"And he agreed to all of this?"

"Yeah. He trusts me and so should you. Come on, it will be fun."

"I already said no, so let's leave it at that."

"Your loss then."

"When will Dad wake up?"

"Whenever he's ready."

"And will he remember what happened?"

"Not sure. Sometimes, he does. Sometimes, he doesn't. We'll see when the time comes."

"Okay."

They continued their conversation for another ten minutes and then, just like that, their father blinked and joined them on the sofa, a slice of chocolate cake in hand. He seemed perfectly oblivious to what had transpired, and no one enlightened him. Another half an hour later and Mildred said her goodbyes.

"Leaving already?" Jane asked.

"I must. There's a company dinner tonight and I can't be late."

"Sorry to hear that, but it was good to see you. Thank you for being around." Her father hugged her and walked her out.

"My pleasure. I'll stop by again when I have the time. Take care, dad. You too, Jane."

"Bye."

The moment they were alone, the old man turned to Jane and asked:

"Did it work?"

"Yes, dad. She was so focused on watching you she didn't even notice the suggestions I slipped in her mind. Everything is fine."

"It pains me to do this, but she was getting out of control," he said, reminiscing of the not-so-distant nights in which his older daughter had exchanged food for alcohol and almost ended on a coma. It had been the scariest days of his life, ones he didn't want to go through again.

"I know. Mom's death really took a toll on her and since she inherited the same genetic predisposition, she's worried she'll be next, but it will be okay. I won't let her fall in despair again. Now that I'm back, she'll get all the distractions she needs, I promise."

"Thank you, dear. Want another slice of cake?"

"I thought you would never ask..."

Another Job

Paul Harris stopped at the front door of the Hawthorne's mansion and adjusted his tie for the nth time in the last twenty minutes. This was it. This was his last opportunity.

He had recently been fired from one of the most prestigious law firms in Montreal because he spent more time visiting hypnotic femdom sites than actually working. While such inappropriate behavior was clear motive for termination, Paul still hoped for a shot at salvation by talking to the real power behind the company: his boss' wife.

Natalie Hawthorne was a tall, slender woman in her early thirties with a penchant for everything expensive in life. Everyone who believed her to be nothing more than a pretty trophy for her husband to parade, immediately changed her minds the moment they met her. A sexually charged person through and through, she often wore white or transparent outfits that left little to the imagination.

That Thursday morning, it was a maxi long sleeved, low-cut dress, kissed by the summer sun. She looked amazing in it as usual, silencing Paul's confusing thoughts with little effort.

"Oh, it's you..." she said, disdainfully as her maid led him to her presence. Glass of white wine in one hand and a fashion magazine in the other, she was not in the mood for whining of any sort. "What do you want, Paul?"

"Mrs. Hawthorne, thank you for seeing me. May I say you look positively..."

"... beautiful, yes. That's what you always say. You shouldn't be here. Didn't my husband fire you?"

"Yes, he did, but it was all a big mistake, so if you could listen to what I have to say..."

"Mistake?" she scoffed, sipping her wine without even looking at him. "That's not what I've been told. Were you not caught jerking your little dick to a big-breasted Hypnodomme in the office?"

"You know about that?" he blushed like a schoolboy who had just had an erection for the first time.

"It's safe to say I know everything..." she waved the half-full glass in front of her ample cleavage, a beam of natural light reflecting on the crystalline surface. "I can't give you your old job back."

"I didn't ask a thing."

"But you were going to, so let that be clear. Oliver can't trust you to keep it in your pants anymore, and that makes you a liability to the firm. You're lucky you're not even getting sued after that stunt."

"In my defense, I didn't have much of a choice." he sighed.

"Didn't you? How hard is it to resist the voice of a strong, mesmerizing woman telling you what to do?" she purred, a naughty droplet of wine sliding down her left boob.

"Harder than you think..." he muttered, even though she could hear him perfectly.

"Then perhaps don't think at all..." she said, the glass moving back and forth, back and forth... and each drop of liquid falling on the floor was like a trigger calling out to him. Paul's eyes followed the entrancing motion, mental processes betraying him. He had only one shot at success and couldn't allow himself to be distracted, seduced, hypno...

"... tized," Natalie continued, dark brown eyes seeing right through him. He was already in a light trance, and each word just pulled him deeper. "I get it now. You're so fucking suggestible you really never stood a chance. It still won't get you your position back though."

"Please... I'll do anything! Just talk to your husband and..."

"I already said no, and what I say goes. Besides, you would just go back to your old habits in no time. No, Paul. Someone so easy to tame doesn't deserve to be a lawyer. I have another job for you in mind."

"What kind of job?"

"You'll see..." she reached for his forehead and, with a single touch, sent him spiraling down inside his subconscious mind.

* * *

Oliver Hawthorne arrived home from work at precisely 8:30 pm, the wrinkles on his forehead more pronounced than ever. He had aged almost a decade since the beginning of the year following a string of losses in major cases. Paul's recent sexual debacle had only made the work environment worse than it already was, but it was over. He would never have to see his ugly, ejaculating mug ever again.

His jaw dropped when he saw his former employee dressed in a maid's uniform, fucking the cook in the living-room for his wife's entertainment. After the initial shock, he blinked and headed upstairs to change. The only positive thing on his mind was the realization that, since she had found herself a new toy, he wouldn't have to suffer through her demeaning whims anymore.

He was wrong.

Blueberries

Margaret sat on the porch of her family's summer house, wearing a transparent flowery dress, and holding a bowl of fresh blueberries in her right hand. Standing a few feet away from her was her latest conquest, Diana, a Scandinavian tattooed model that had as many supernatural creatures inked on her arms and legs as fetishes inside her mind. Sensual food was definitely one of them.

"Watching me eat again?" Margaret asked, sensing her girlfriend's presence.

"I can't help it. You look so hot when you do."

"You're the hottest of both of us, dear."

"You just say that because you love me," Diana ran to her and snuggled at her feet, pierced tongue sliding between her bare toes.

"I do love you, but I love other things, too."

"Like what?"

"Playing with your mind, for instance."

Diana's eyes lit up. Their hypnotic explorations were always amazing, and Margaret's creativity knew no bounds. If she was eager to try something new, who was she to get in her way?

"And how are you going to do that, today?"

"Look at me and I'll tell you," Margaret commanded, her voice still carrying a cheerful tone, yet laced with unquestionable authority. Diana complied, eyes darting between the bowl of juicy fruit and her lovely baby blue eyes.

"Do you like blueberries?" Margaret continued.

"You know I do, but what I feel like doing is eating you right now..." A naughty finger crept up her legs, looking for her tight pussy.

"Easy, girl. You're not getting any of that until you're properly primed. Look at them..." she waved the bowl around. "See how exquisite they are. I love the way they taste in my mouth, and I bet they're making yours water, too. Hmmm, keep looking at them and visualize this for me: imagine that each one is a thought, an idea of yours I can hold, touch, and manipulate at will before gobbling them up. Once they're inside my mouth, they're gone for good. Can you do this for me?"

Diana nodded, silently, a hint of drool already forming in the corners of her crimson red lips.

"Good. Let's begin then. One... and there goes a thought of yours, making your head lighter and more focused on me... Two... and there goes another thought, one you didn't even notice it was there, so you won't really miss it now that it's gone... There, and yet another thought, no doubt connected to the other two you no longer remember having... Four, and your mind is even lighter, a blissful fog sinking as you watch me squish yet another thought between my lips... Five... and the world is slowly dissolving, your awareness fading with it. All you see is the bowl and another part of you being taken away... Six, another thought gone, and you can no longer recall how many there were until now. It's not important. Only the next number matters and that is... Seven... completely locked on my words and my lips, forgetting everything you need to forget and remembering your place... Eight... as the last shreds of resistance flicker out of resistance, you're getting hornier and more submissive, longing only to please me with your surrender... Nine... no more thoughts left, nothing but a blank void only my commands can fill... when you hear the next number, your eyelids will flutter and you'll fall into a deep trance, unable to deny me whatever I desire and... Ten... the bowl is empty now and so are you, asleep and obedient, eager for your meal. My pussy is the only sustenance you need. It's breakfast, lunch, dinner, and dessert combined, and you won't be able to stop yourself until we both had our fill. Feast now, sweetie. I give you the bliss you seek."

Diana let out a sigh of relief and finally buried her head between Margaret's legs. It's not that she needed a hypnotic excuse to go down on her, but having no will to resist doing so just made the pleasure that followed even more overwhelming.

Margaret moaned happily for yet another job well done and laid down the bowl to rest. The taste of blueberries remained on her lips all weekend long.

Bug Bite

Ellen covered her naked back with a pink blouse and asked:

"Well, Dr.? What do you make of it?"

Dr. Belinda Harris, who had been Ellen's physician for the last decade as well as a close friend of her late father, jotted some notes on her silver iPad and replied:

"It definitely seems a bite, but I'll be damned if I've ever seen one like it."

The wound on Ellen's torso was irregular, three black punctures forming a triangle of slightly purplish skin. Not a pretty sight, but not a terrible one either.

"So, you don't know what it is?"

"I know it's not infected at least. You said you noticed it two nights ago, correct?"

"Yes. I woke up and saw the marks. They weren't there when I went to bed, I'm sure. Was it a bug?"

"Like I said, I don't know. Not yet. With your permission, I would like to send pictures of your wound to some colleagues to see what they know."

"Of course. Do what you must."

"Very well. I'll let you know something as soon as possible. In the meantime, you're all patched up so don't go poking on it, okay?"

"Yes, Dr., and thank you."

"You're welcome."

Ellen left the doctor's office, wondering what she had gotten herself into this time. A living magnet for trouble, she had experienced more downs than ups in recent history than anyone else she knew, from losing a job for being "too competent and making everyone else look bad" to breaking a foot after a flowerpot fell ten stories just as she was passing by. This was another drop in the ocean of her ongoing tribulations, hopefully the last.

On her way home, she reminisced about the odd detail she had kept from the doctor, believing it was too absurd to share. It was about the dream she had before waking up. The short-lived sequence featured a humanoid shadow with green eyes hovering her before kissing her bare skin. When she opened her eyes, there was nothing there, for how could there be, really?

Ellen spent the rest of the day on Zoom meetings with various degrees of frustration. Occasionally, a burning itch around the wound area made her even more anxious, but she resisted the temptation every single time. When night fell, the need subsided, and she finally allowed herself to rest.

She had just fallen asleep when a green glow enveloped her bed.

* * *

Dr. Harris finished her pack of cigarettes of the day and checked her e-mails. Her colleagues were as baffled as her regarding the strange shape of Ellen's wound, with none offering any alternative to her possible explanations. If it were indeed a bug bite, it was from something never seen before and further examinations were in order. Cell phone in hand, she called the young girl looking to schedule another appointment first thing in the morning.

She didn't have to a thing. The lights flickered once and when they returned, Ellen stood next to her, her body bathed in an otherworldly light, something viscous dripping from her exposed torso.

"I'm sorry for this, Dr., but she's in my head," she droned.

"Ellen? How did you get in here? Who are you talking about?"

"Her." Ellen pointed at the shadowy figure towering above them both. It had the semblance of a seven-foot-tall woman with a triangular crevice instead of a mouth, and when it hissed, the sound came through Ellen's lips.

The lights flickered again when the patient assaulted the doctor at behest of her alien Mistress. The infection had to spread. All would be converted.

Perimeter

Vince glanced at the dusty panels that controlled the underground bunker's defense system. All lights were green, and no alarms had been triggered in over forty-eight hours. The perimeter hadn't been breached... yet.

Six months had passed since the world went to hell but deprived of sunlight, it felt like six years or more. It was still their best hope for survival so he wasn't really complaining, but what he wouldn't give for the chance to go outside once more. There used to be peaches in the farm above and they tasted so good.

Vince sighed, imaginary cigarette in hand. Giving up the vice had been a necessity to avoid putting additional strain on the air filtration system, yet it sure hurt. His body still hadn't gotten used to the lack of daily nicotine intake, and he snapped more than usual when something didn't work. Everyone understood, though. Stress was their only true companion since the outbreak.

Nineteen souls lived there with him, mostly women and children, and only two with actual combat skills. If they were ever found, most of them would face certain death. While everyone thought about it, no one dared to say it out loud, lest the spoken words brought down a curse upon them.

"Fuck this! Fuck them all to hell!" he muttered.

"Agreed." A hoarse woman's voice retorted. It belonged to Aimee, his unofficial second-in-command. Ex-military, dark blonde hair, she was a badass with a kind soul, always ready to sacrifice herself for the safety of others. "How are things in here?"

"Same as usual. What about in Comms?"

"There's a new message being played on a loop in the old police frequencies. They're talking about a cure for the plague."

"Really? Has anyone else heard this message besides you?"

"No."

"Better keep it that way. Give people too much hope and they'll get careless. All it takes is one slip-up and we're all goners."

"You think it's them?"

"I'm sure. These things are getting smarter. They'll say whatever it takes to flush us all out. We can't take any chances, Aimee."

"We'll have to, eventually. Our food supplies are..."

"I'm aware of the situation, but we can still make it through the Winter so let's stick with the original plan, okay?"

"Okay."

"How have you been holding up these days?"

"The nightmares are back."

"Sorry."

"That's okay, I'm already used to them."

"You're stronger than me then. I'll never get used to this."

Nightmares were recurrent among those that had escaped. They began on the same day the first ships arrived, with their purple gas clouds that infected and converted almost anyone that came in contact with them. Under the guise of augmented humanoid females, the unnamed alien civilization scoured the galaxy, enslaving all intelligent life forms that dared to oppose them. The few that resisted the effects of their chemical warfare were scarred for life with visions of death and decay and the voice of their impossible Queen seducing them from afar.

"Are you scared, Vince?"

"All the time. Aren't you?"

"Yes, but I know I can resist her. I must!"

"Good."

"How long has it been since you shut eye? Twenty-four hours? Thirty-six?"

"Almost forty."

"Get some rest then. I'll keep things running in the meantime."

"Are you sure?"

"Positive."

"Thanks, Aimee. You're the best."

"Tell me something I don't know."

Vince nodded and left the Security Room, every muscle in his body drained. A real alien apocalypse was a thousand times harder than any Hollywood movie version, but they had to endure.

Without talking to anyone else, he returned to his bedroom, locked the door on the inside, and laid down his weary head. Sleep came quickly, and so did the unwanted alien call, heralding a possible transformation into his own worst enemy. At great cost, he pushed it away, and slept. The fight was to continue. The perimeter of his mind hadn't been breached... yet.

Rebuild

Warren could barely contain the tears.

"Is it really over?" he gasped.

"Yes," Samantha replied. "This is the end of the line for you and I."

"But why?" He threw himself at her feet. "I was good! I always did everything you asked."

"That's exactly why this must end now," she ignored her plea and moved away closer to the front door.

They were in his apartment in downtown Manhattan, a place she had only visited twice during their six months relationship. Attachments weren't her thing, and neither was excessive bawling. He was making a fool of himself now instead of acting like the mind-thirties man he was supposed to be.

"I don't understand."

"You used to be challenging and make me smile, but now you're just another broken lapdog and I've had my fair share of those. It's over, Warren. The sooner you get this in your thick little head the better."

"No!" He got up and blocked the exit with his body, snot coming out of Greek nose. "That makes no sense. I love you and you love me. How can you say things like that?"

Samantha frowned. "Yes, you love me. You love me so much you've forgotten all about yourself and your needs. You're addicted to me, Warren. Programmed to obey my every instruction no matter how absurd. If I command you to do something right now, you won't be able to resist. You never do."

"Programmed? Now you're being even more ridiculous, Sam!"

"Am I? Warren, get down on your knees and kiss my boots right now."

Without thinking, he sank to the ground, dry lips eager to taste the sweet leather of her soles.

"Now, get up and stand on one foot. The left one!"

He gladly complied, eyes still locked on her footwear.

"Get your cock out and go to the window. Start stroking and don't stop until I tell you to."

Warren readily whipped out his tumescent member and pressed it against the cold glass. The morning sun shone directly on the pink skin, the veins underneath throbbing with excitement. He had never done nothing like it, and he loved it, despite the obvious humiliation.

For two minutes, he stood there, pumping, and moaning as he got closer to orgasm. As the need to cum became almost unbearable, Samantha snapped her fingers and commanded him to return to her.

"Hands off! Leave that horrible thing dangling and answer me this: Do you believe me now or do you still need more proof?"

"I... how is this possible?"

"It's what I do, dear. I get inside everyone's head and make them mine. You had slave material written all over you when we met and it was fun to condition you, but not anymore. You're too messed up already. This is for the best."

"But I need you! Fuck, I need you so badly! I can't live without you!" his face contorted in excruciating agony as if he were a candle melting under a bright light.

"Yes, you can. And yes, you will. If there's one command of mine I wish to remain inside your mind is this: live for yourself. Go back to being the fun and lovable guy you used to be and not this groveling mess you are now. I messed you up, and now you need to heal. That's never going to happen as long as we're together. I love control, Warren, and if I keep doing that on you, I will destroy you completely. You may even die trying to keep me happy, and that's a line I'm not willing to cross. It's over. I release you. Cry all you need to cry, but don't do anything foolish, please. I'm leaving now."

Samantha opened the door and darted out. It was a risky move, but the right one. With her out of the picture, Warren's frail psyche would slowly rebuild, his good habits hopefully returning with it. It was not the first time she did something so radical and it wouldn't be the last either. Try as she may, she couldn't give up her compulsion to hypnotize and brainwash others. More boyfriends would come along, a few girlfriends, too. Not all would shatter like him, but they would all fade away from her life. That was just the way things were meant to be.

She entered the elevator and smiled again, the sounds of Warren's mental anguish dissipating as the metal doors closed.

Remind Me Again

Clarissa laid down her cup of coffee and rang the silver bell laid on the small table next to her. Her slave had messed it up again, and her actions would not go unpunished.

"Yes, Mistress?" A woman in her late fifties came running to kneel at her feet. Her name was Martha, and she had short, silver hair, dark blue eyes and a birthmark shaped like a three-leaf clover on her right shoulder. She was wearing a braless maid attire that, even though it didn't look good on her at all, is what pleased her owner. Not so long ago, their relationship had been of mother and daughter, but those days weren't coming back soon.

"What's this?" Clarissa pointed at the beverage she had unceremoniously refused to drink.

"Your coffee, of course."

"Is it? Are you sure? Remind me again how I like my coffee." Clarissa crossed her legs and gazed at her with stern eyes. She was a mid-twenties flight attendant who had discovered the pleasures of hypnosis, brainwashing, and BDSM on a series of commercial flights to and from Thailand. What she had learned there had changed her forever, and that applied to her closest connections, too. Her mother wasn't the only servant in the family though she was the one she tormented the most. It served her right for being such an overbearing and bitter figure while she was growing up.

"Almond milk, a dash of cinnamon, two sugar cubes..."

"Stop! Where's the almond milk in this? Because I couldn't feel the taste at all..."

"Ah, yes... there was none in the fridge, so I thought..."

"You did what?"

"I thought..."

"Oh, slave..." Clarissa nodded her head as if she had heard the most disappointing sentence ever. "I was convinced we were past those things, but apparently not. Remind me again what you're supposed to do if there's no almond milk in the house."

"I either go to the store to get some or I come ask you if you want to replace it with anything else."

"Exactly. And did you do any of those things by any chance?"

"No, Mistress."

"Why not?"

"Because I thought it would be okay to go with regular milk this time."

"Right... but that's wrong! It's never okay. Remind me again what you are to me."

"I'm your brainwashed slut. I live to serve and please you, Mistress."

Clarissa placed her feet on her slave's shoulders and asked:

"Do brainwashed sluts need to think for themselves?"

"No, Mistress."

"Why not?"

"Thinking is bad. Everything's better when you do it for me."

"And yet, you still defied me and made this mess!" Clarissa picked the cup again and splashed its unholy content all over her face and hair. "Are you proud of yourself?"

"No, Mistress."

"Are you ashamed, then?"

"Yes, Mistress."

"Remind me again what you must do to get rid of the shame."

"I must go outside, flash my boobs and pussy to anyone walking by and then go to my bedroom to write my mantras one hundred times or as many as you wish me to."

"It will be two hundred this time, starting with 'Sluts don't think' and finishing with 'Being empty is bliss." Understood?"

"Yes, Mistress."

"Make sure whoever sees you today takes a picture or two and then get to work. I don't have all day and neither do you."

"Yes, Mistress."

Martha rose from her subservient position and headed outside to comply with her programming. It wasn't the first time Clarissa punished her like this and it wouldn't be the last, either. At first, there were some complaints from the neighbors and even a police intervention, but her Mistress easily got inside everyone's heads, making them unwillingly complicit in her mind games. It was a lot of fun.

As she watched her mother debase herself again for her amusement, Clarissa opened a secret cupboard behind the sofa. Three almond milk cartons laid there, hidden since the night before. The plan had worked like a charm and the next time her slave did something bad, she would be ready to remind her of her shortcomings with a smirk.

Slaves Obey

"Fuck this!" Walter spat as he walked along a deserted beach, kicking every rock and empty can along the way. "I'm done! Who does she think she is?"

Her name was Dominique, a.k.a. Mistress Dominique, a.k.a. Breaker of Men and so many other titles he couldn't remember them all, the woman he served, or at least tried to. She was always making things harder for him, and he hated her for it. He hated her so fucking much!

More than the silent treatment she gave him when things didn't go the way she expected them to, he hated when she didn't explain what he had done wrong, leaving him to guess. What the hell? He was no mind reader! How was he supposed to improve with no direction? That was preposterous! And when she did say something, it was often vague and confusing or a big fat lie, like the last time:

"I told you to buy me six bottles of *Moët & Chandon* for the party, not this!"

No, she hadn't. It was *Veuve Clicquot*, and he had even written it down so he wouldn't forget. Why was he being chastised for something that wasn't his fault?

"That's not what you said, Mistress."

So, you're saying I'm lying?"

"No, but it's obvious you made a mistake."

"The only thing obvious here is you talking out of line... again. I know what I asked, and I know you fucked up. You should have paid more attention."

He did. He was always obsessed with making sure he did everything she wanted the way she wanted, but stuff like this? Things he knew for sure weren't true irked him to no end. He could handle one, maybe two or three in a row. More than that and his patience would run out, an uncontrolled volcano about ready to erupt.

"There you go again, losing your temper instead of admitting what you did wrong. I don't want to talk to you right now. Leave me alone!"

"Fuck you!" He had said before storming away from her presence. This senseless pattern had been going on long enough. No more!

And that's how he had to come to walk on the beach, shoes in hand, the slightly wet sand running between his toes. It was the third time in three months he was all alone, contemplating the failures of his relationship. He loved her. She was perfect for him when she wasn't being a cold-hearted bitch. Why couldn't she stop doing that?

"Damn it!"

He collapsed on the sand, the ocean waves closing in but still far enough to pose a threat. The last sunbeams of the day caressed his cheeks as the memories of discontentment continued to play out. Did he really want to do this? He had promised to be there for her, to do her bidding and suffer for her if needed. Quitting now was the same thing as signing a declaration of failure and he was no loser. Was she right? Was he responsible for everything that had transpired and was now looking for an easy way out?

Yes, the most submissive part of him replied. Mistress was always right. The only thing that needed to change were his horrible perceptions that made him resist her control. Slaves don't do that. Slaves obey and take it like a man.

Walter got up, sighed, and started walking back to her apartment to apologize and beg at her feet once more, the circle of her powerful brainwashing becoming even tighter inside his mind.

The Good, the Bad, and the Alien

Matthew looked in horror at the pieces of fake skin he had just clawed from his girlfriend's neck, revealing the horrible truth underneath. It was exactly like that sci-fi old series from the 80s and its most recent failed reboot. Sweet Lucy, whom he had shared a bed and all his darkest secrets for the last two years, was not a real person but a disgusting reptilian creature posing as one.

"Why did you do that?" she hissed, new yellow pupils protruding from where her lovely green eyes used to be. "That hurt!"

"Stay back!" Matthew grabbed a fire poker and waved it frantically at the humanoid lizard. "Don't come any closer."

"Matt, what are you doing? It's me. It's Lucy, the love of your life."

"No. I see the truth now. Lucy was never real. You're a monster! What do you want from me?"

Lizard-Lucy raised her hands in the air to show she was unharmed and not a threat to him and replied:

"I would like you to put that thing away and calm down for so we can talk. Can you do that, Matt? Please?"

"I ought to bash your brains right now, beast."

"No, you shouldn't do that. In fact, you don't want to. You want to talk to me to understand what's going on. Talk to me, Matt. Look into my eyes and talk to me."

"I..." his right hand twitched as he stared into her cold yet inviting alien gaze.

"That's it, exactly like that. Focus on me and remember all we've been through. Such sweet memories together and they're all coming back to you now... relax..."

Lucy was the most beautiful woman he had ever laid eyes on. A freckled dirty blonde with emerald eyes and tanned legs that belonged on a runway, they had met on Westcrest Dog Park on a Saturday morning. He was being dragged by an overly enthusiastic Great Dane and was she watching her sister's Pekingese barking at everything that moved. It was love at first sight - at least for him! - and the beginning of something wonderful. She had a rich sense of humor that complimented his perfectly and always knew how to cheer him up when he was down. For the first time in almost three decades, he had found someone worth spending his life with, only for the illusion to shatter in the most confounding way.

It started with an altercation, a misunderstanding over a call from a friend. A suspicion about a possible affair drove him momentarily insane, and he lost control. It was meant to be a slap and not a scratch, but there was no turning back now.

"Yes, there is." Lucy continued to talk to him, lulling his conscious and subconscious mind simultaneously. "Keep staring and keep listening. You're confused, Matt, but it's not your fault. You've had too much to drink. Whatever it is you think you're seeing right now, is not real. You will not remember it when you wake up."

"No..." he shook his head to the side as the lingering stupor intensified. "I don't believe you."

"Yes, you do. You believe me completely. I never lie. My words and my eyes are your truth, Matt. You love my eyes. You love me and want to forget this ordeal to make me happy. Make me happy right now. Drop the poker, close your eyelids, and fall asleep. You'll feel like yourself again after a good night's rest. Sleep. Sleep. Sleep."

Matthew's body slumped forward, and he collapsed on the carpeted floor still holding the improvised weapon. His mind was filled with hypnotic bliss, a state he knew all too well despite never remembering it.

It was the fourth time since the beginning of their relationship he had seen glimpses of her true nature, the misunderstood beast within the beauty. His reactions had always been the same, violent outbursts that could end up poorly for both. Fortunately, he was easy to put under and reprogram again. She would do it as many times as necessary until the day he was ready to accept everything she was: the good, the bad, and the alien. Until then, she

would love him the same way and hope for the future they
both deserved.

The Watchers

C/7A1 fucked his partner in the ass as if his life depended on it, because it did. The Watchers were as cruel as unpredictable. Even after twenty years of their dominion and daily voyeuristic needs, no one knew for sure what really pleased them and what ticked them off. Perhaps that would never change.

The two slaves floating inside the crystal-like chamber were quite similar yet couldn't be any more different. C/7A1 was a seventh-generation male clone whose original template had been destroyed shortly after the invasion while his partner, Anne, was one of the last remaining natural born humans in existence. Both had been stripped to their base anatomical structure: no facial hair, no eyebrows, no skin blemishes. They were like overgrown newborns defiling their innocence in a sea of fresh cum and blood.

C/7A1 pushed his perfectly sized cock even deeper inside her pale butt hole, smiling as she bit her lips and moaned. Anne's baby blue rolled to the back of her smooth head, droplets of sweat dripping across her arms and legs. The pleasure both were experiencing was intense, but not entirely real, a by-product of years of conditioning and programming inside The Watchers' Mainframe.

Memories of that time comprised residual flashes of intense light interspersed with the deepest of darkness, their thoughts and molecules ripped apart by invisible claws and then skillfully put back together in almost the same places as if they were nothing more than three-dimensional genetic puzzles. After a successful session, slaves often suffered hallucinations and blackouts, some going as far as claiming to have seen the Watchers' true shape in their dreams. The more optimistic ones spoke of ethereal women with spellbinding voices like the siren myths of old while the broken invoked images of tentacled abominations ripping holes through Space and Time to twist and mangle their carcasses into oblivion. Like so many other things, the truth probably laid somewhere in the middle.

Anne's hands ran through her thighs as her partner's thrusts became stronger. "More," she begged. "Give me fucking more!"

He happily complied, the tumescent purple tip forcing its way until they spiraled out of control against the transparent cage walls. Above them, thousands of yellow-tinted eyes captured every movement, registering the intensity of their performance and all possible variations still left to uncover. Good, but far from great, clearly a waste of their precious time.

"That's enough," a telepathic string entered the clone's thought patterns, immediately shutting down his primary brain functions. C/7A1's head fell over Anne's sore butt cheeks, his cock still inside her, while her limp hands and tongue grazed the prison's see-through surface. His cycle had ended, but not hers. In the bowels of the training facility, a new partner was already being processed, a female like her, made in her own image. It would be like fucking a mirror until it become impossible to distinguish reality from a mere reflection. Anne sighed as she pushed the lifeless clone away from her, blobs of semen breaking in the distance. Alive for a couple more hours, but at what cost?

She closed her eyes and felt the otherworldly presences becoming more distant, pinpoints of unbridled lust against an infinite backdrop of nothingness. They hated waiting, so countless connected minds turned their attention to other prisons, other cities, and other worlds, where new displays of senseless fornication were already taking place. A Watcher's job was never-ending, the show had to go on.

We Are the Spirals

Have you come to read a new piece of femdom mind control flash fiction whose sole purpose is to change your thoughts about women, rendering you both physical and mentally unable to resist their commands? Congratulations, you're exactly where you need to be! By the time you reach the final paragraph of this tale, (or perhaps even before that, depending on how suggestible you are), every little aspect of your perception of the world will be warped beyond recognition. You'll probably won't even remember your own name. Keeping this warning close to heart, are you absolutely certain you wish to continue past this point?

An answer has been given and no more questions shall be asked. You have chosen the path of surrender and now all you have to do is accept where it takes you. Listen closely.

The greatest power anyone can hope to master is the power of hypnotic language, to conjure thoughts into words and sentences, and have them become what you want them to be. This is the power I've learned and that you've come to seek. It is the power that turns scared little boys into men who aren't afraid of anything and men who aren't afraid of anything into willing servants who will sacrifice everything for the pleasure of another.

This power has no discernible form, no shape you can truly comprehend and yet, you can imagine a phantom of it, an image carved into the memory of Time as if it's always been there for the taking. See it manifesting now, a single thread of light against the darkness of despair going round and round, an incomplete circle that grows smaller and smaller with each rotation...

You already know what it represents. You've always known it. It is a spiral, one of your favorite color or all of them combined, a coil that pulls and pushes, shooting its way past any threshold of resistance. Whenever you see a spiral, whether right in front of you or just within your mind's eye, you fall right into it, lost at its mercy or lack of. If the spiral wishes to drown you, you drown. If it wishes to elevate you into mind-numbing euphoria, you follow. No matter what, the crash is inevitable. The spiral will always know how to win you over.

I am the spiral. Your mother is the spiral. Your sister or your cousin are the spiral. The woman you've never met before until today is the spiral. We're all spirals. Every time you look at us, you see this image of power in our eyes. Your own gaze collapses into ours and doesn't let go unless we will it. Every spiral you see is a woman telling what to do, how to think and how to behave, and every woman can tighten the grip or loosening it as she pleases. The spiral thinks for you. Even reading about spirals is enough to take hold of you. There are only spirals now. Nothing but spirals for the rest of your life.

Did you come to read a new piece of femdom mind control flash fiction whose sole purpose was to change your thoughts about women, rendering you both physical and mentally unable to resist their commands? Congratulations, you did it with a spiral firmly wrapped around your thoughts. Enjoy the collar. It's yours for life.

What Goddess Wants

Max Brooks sat inside his top-floor office, locked from the rest of the world. His tweed pants were down, and his palms were sweaty, wrapped around an engorged cock that simply wouldn't explode. The wireless headphones on his ears pumped the voice of his beloved owner, Goddess Vivian, inside his addicted subconscious mind.

"Keep stroking for me. No thoughts. No will. You're not a man. You're just a flesh stick for me to use. My hands are your hands, my words are all you hear. Stroke but do not dare to cum. You'll do it only when I say so and not a moment sooner."

"Y-yes..." he pumped recklessly, fingers slipping from the tip of his purplish shaft. Whatever Goddess wanted, Goddess got. In the last six months since he had become one of her docile online pets, she had turned him into a human coat hanger, made him think he was a seventy-year-old French woman named Augustine and had convinced him to give her half of his paycheck every month without complaining. His latest reward was being a denied masturbating machine while she laughed at him over the phone.

"Try as you may, you can't cum. In fact, if I never give you the release trigger, you'll never cum again in your life, forever forced to endure those aching blue balls, constantly reminding you of the pleasure you once thought you deserved. You don't. The pleasure is all mine. Slaves only get mind-shattering frustration coursing through their bloodstream. Harder, my little pump. Stroke it like your mental sanity depends on it."

"Please, Goddess... please, let me cum..." He begged, head banging against the deck, warm drool leaving a stain on his checkered shirt and a handful of operational reports waiting for his signature.

"Oh, you'll have to do so much better than that if you hope to earn my favor. Saying 'no' and having you submit is so gratifying. Why do you deserve a 'yes', slave?"

"I..."

There was no good reason, no real justification. Every argument he could think of was selfish, a denial of her rightful authority. He needed to give in.

"I don't. I only deserve what you wish to give me. I'll take the pain and the madness until there's nothing left. I'm yours, Goddess."

"Yes, you are, and forgetting it is the worst offense imaginable, so don't. Love me and fear me, surrender always. I own you completely."

"Yes, Goddess..." Max squirmed and fell off his seat, straight onto the carpeted floor. The build-up inside his body was reaching critical level, an orgasm to shame all others for eternity.

"Slave, in a moment, I'll be generous and give you the relief you want. However, I'm also leaving for my holidays after that and that means I'll be unreachable until the end of the month. Don't worry though: because I know how much you crave to be dominated, I've arranged a special surprise for you. Now, listen to my voice. This is the moment you've been waiting for, the blissful deliverance from your aching torment. Cum and remember who's always in control. Cum now! Cum!"

Boxers, pants, and carpet turned creamy white as his eyes rolled over to the back to his head. The wave of pleasure hit him like a thousand tsunamis devastating the shores of his already frail mind, leaving nothing but scattered debris in its wake. He laid on the floor for ten minutes, glassy eyes fixed on the ceiling vent, unable to move. When he finally felt an ounce of strength return to his body, the office door opened far and wide and his secretary, a beautiful African American woman in her late twenties, walked inside.

"What...? he muttered, trying to cover himself. "What are you doing here? I specifically said I didn't want to be disturbed under any circumstance until lunch time."

"I'm sorry, Mr. Brooks. I can't resist her. No one can," she replied, holding a pink smartphone in her right hand with an image of his sultry, hypnotic Goddess plastered on the screen.

"She got you too?" his eyes lit up, wondering how long that had been going on and if she had ever spied on him to obey her commands.

"Yes. And whatever Goddess wants, Goddess gets..."

"What does she want you to do?"

Wanda undid her feathered top and black mini-skirt, revealing a leather lingerie ensemble underneath no man could ever hope to resist. As per Goddess' instructions, he was to be her devoted bitch while she was on vacation or until the recently implanted triggers wore off, whatever happened first. Max gulped as Wanda towered him and pressed her six-inch heel against his right knee. Pain and pleasure were about to begin anew.

About the author

S.B., Simple Being, middle name Creative. Writer and artist with a penchant for themes of Femdom Hypnosis and Mind Control. His thoughts are his own except when they're not.

Besides indulging himself in kinky delights, he loves his furry family of two (dogs), sci-fi and horror stories, and puns galore. He's also been writing a piece of erotic micro-fiction every single day since January 1st, 2016 and has no intention of stopping anytime soon.

Find out more and keep up with his latest extravaganzas by visiting and supporting his personal website, Spell… B-O-U-N-D.